W9-BRR-655

The Boxcar Children Mysteries

THE BOXCAR CHILDREN
SURPRISE ISLAND
THE YELLOW HOUSE MYSTERY
MYSTERY RANCH
MIKE'S MYSTERY
BLUE BAY MYSTERY
THE WOODSHED MYSTERY
THE LIGHTHOUSE MYSTERY
MOUNTAIN TOP MYSTERY
SCHOOLHOUSE MYSTERY
CABOOSE MYSTERY
HOUSEBOAT MYSTERY
SNOWBOUND MYSTERY
TREE HOUSE MYSTERY
BICYCLE MYSTERY
MYSTERY IN THE SAND
MYSTERY BEHIND THE WALL
BUS STATION MYSTERY
BENNY UNCOVERS A MYSTERY
THE HAUNTED CABIN MYSTERY
THE DESERTED LIBRARY MYSTERY
THE ANIMAL SHELTER MYSTERY
THE OLD MOTEL MYSTERY
THE MYSTERY OF THE HIDDEN PAINTING
THE AMUSEMENT PARK MYSTERY
THE MYSTERY OF THE MIXED-UP ZOO

THE MYSTERY OF THE MIXED-UP ZOO

created by
GERTRUDE CHANDLER WARNER

Illustrated by Charles Tang

SCHOLASTIC INC.
New York Toronto London Auckland Sydney

No part of this publication may be reproduced in whole or in part, or stored in a retrieval system, or transmitted in any form or by any means, electronic, mechanical, photocopying, recording, or otherwise, without written permission of the publisher. For information regarding permission, write to Albert Whitman & Company, 6340 Oakton Street, Morton Grove, IL 60053-2723.

ISBN 0-590-45373-4

Copyright © 1992 by Albert Whitman & Company. All rights reserved. Published by Scholastic Inc., 730 Broadway, New York, NY 10003, by arrangement with Albert Whitman & Company. THE BOXCAR CHILDREN is a registered trademark of Albert Whitman & Company.

16 15 14 13 12 11 10 9 8 7   2 3 4 5 6 7/9

Printed in the U.S.A.   28

First Scholastic printing, March 1992

Contents

CHAPTER 1

Edward Marlow

Driving down the highway, James Alden pointed out the sign announcing the city of Rosedale to his four grandchildren, Henry, Jessie, Violet, and Benny.

"There's where my old friend, Edward Marlow, lives."

Benny, the youngest, craned his neck. "I see it!" he said in an excited voice.

"I can't wait to meet Mr. Marlow," Jessie said. "Did you go to school with him?"

Grandfather chuckled. "He was my college roommate. Edward dreamed up all kinds of excitement. He had a lot of pep in those days." He paused. "I'm eager to see him. I haven't seen him for years. He's owned this small zoo for a long time, and I want to see how he's getting along."

"Is he as handsome as you, Grandfather?" Violet asked with a smile.

Grandfather laughed. "Edward was a good-looking boy with a mischievous streak."

"Edward sounds like fun!" Benny said. "And his zoo even more fun!"

"Yes, he does," Henry agreed. "How far does he live from the zoo, Grandfather?"

"He lives just one block away, just a short walk," Grandfather said.

Smiling, Violet leaned back in the seat. She brushed back her hair so she'd look her best for Grandfather's friend.

Jessie smiled at her sister. Her thick hair was tangled from the wind, but she smoothed it down and tied it back with a ribbon.

"I wish we could have brought Watch," Benny said.

"Watch will be fine," Henry said. "You know how Mrs. McGregor spoils our dog."

Benny nodded, satisfied.

More and more highway signs appeared. They knew they were in the city limits when they passed a sign that said:

ROSEDALE, MASSACHUSETTS
POPULATION: 85,000

A motel flashed by, then a few stores, a park, a public swimming pool, and a movie theater. On this hot August day, hundreds of kids were swimming.

Grandfather swung off Highway Six onto Main Street, then drove straight for several blocks. "Watch for Hamilton Street," he said, pushing his sunglasses up on his nose.

"There it is!" Jessie exclaimed. "Hamilton Street."

"Now," Grandfather said, "look for 501 Hamilton."

"Five-oh-one!" yelled Benny a moment later, delighted that he'd been the first to spot Edward's house.

The narrow two-story house was wooden

and quite plain. Not a flower, not a bush grew near it.

Grandfather stopped the station wagon and the children scrambled out.

Grandfather, straight and tall, headed up the walk, and knocked on the door.

The door opened wide and there stood Edward Marlow. He was a gray-haired man with a pink round face. His blue eyes twinkled, and a grin spread across his face. "Come in, come in," he called. "Welcome!"

Grandfather grabbed Edward and the two men hugged one another. "Edward, it's great to see you!" Grandfather said.

"And you, too, you old fox!" Edward said.

Grandfather stepped aside. "Meet my four grandchildren," he said proudly. He pointed to the tallest. "This is Henry, who's the oldest, he's fourteen; Jessie is twelve; Violet is ten; and here's six-year-old Benny."

"How do you do, sir," Benny said, stepping up and shaking Edward's hand.

"You're all to call me Edward," Edward ordered in a teasing tone. "Come into the kitchen for a surprise."

Going through the living room, Jessie noticed piles of newspapers and yellow magazines stacked in the corner. Upon a closer look, she saw that the yellow magazines were all *National Geographic*s. Next to a worn leather chair was a world globe. Edward must like geography, she thought. Tables and lamps were dusty, and a cobweb drifted down from the ceiling.

The dining room appeared to be seldom used. In the center was a heavy round table with six chairs. On one wall was a china cupboard with glass doors so grimy you could hardly see the dishes inside. On the opposite wall was a small table with a telephone and a bench beside it.

Edward led them into the kitchen. "Sit down, sit down," he said heartily. He set a quart of ice cream in the center of the kitchen table. Six bowls, spoons, and napkins completed the table setting.

As Edward dished up the ice cream, Violet glanced around. The sink, filled with dirty dishes, was next to the stove. That, too, needed a good cleaning. When Edward

opened the freezer, frozen food was stacked to the top.

"This tastes good," Benny said. "Except for stopping for lunch, we were on the road all day."

"My, my," Edward said sympathetically. "I'll bet you're tired."

"Where do we sleep?" Benny asked.

Grandfather shook his head. "Benny, be patient. Eat your ice cream."

Benny tipped his bowl. "It's empty," he said. "I've finished."

"How about another scoop?" Edward said, leaning toward Benny.

"Thank you, but I'd better not," Benny said.

"That's right," Violet said, "we don't want to spoil our appetites for supper." She wondered, though, if they would eat here. There was not a sign of a prepared dinner, nothing on the bare countertop nor a pot on the stove.

Suddenly a distant roar interrupted them.

"What was that?" Benny asked, his big brown eyes questioning Edward.

"That's the lions at my zoo," Edward explained. "They are fed at five, but around four they start crying for their dinner."

"Just like someone else I know," Jessie teased, smiling at Benny.

"Grandfather says the zoo is close by," Henry said.

"It is!" Edward said. "It's only a block from here, and when the wind is just right, you can hear birds twittering and elephants trumpeting." He laughed. "I love it!"

"Gee!" Benny exclaimed. "That's exciting. I can't wait to see the animals."

"Tomorrow, bright and early, we'll pay the zoo a visit," Edward promised.

"Oh, good!" Benny said. "I like to watch the monkeys."

"And now," Edward said, scraping back his chair, "let me show you your rooms."

The children followed him upstairs. He led them to two small bedrooms. "This," Edward said, indicating a small room with bunk beds, "is the boys' room."

He crossed the hall. "And this is for you," he said to Violet and Jessie, showing them to a bigger room with a large bed.

"Make yourselves at home," Edward said. "We'll go out to a restaurant about six o'clock." He left, going downstairs.

Jessie, unpacking her suitcase, said, "Violet, I don't think Edward has many home-cooked meals."

"I'm sure of it," Violet said. "We'll have to cook dinner for him."

"That will be fun," Jessie said. "We can do a lot to make this place cozy."

Grandfather would be sleeping on a rollaway bed in Edward's large bedroom off the living room. Once everyone had unpacked and washed, they met by the front door.

"I want to take you out to one of my favorite places," Edward said.

They drove to Rita's Restaurant. As soon as they walked in, the woman at the cash register called, "Edward! How are you? Do you want your usual table?"

"Not tonight, Rita. I need a table for six," he replied.

"Can do," she said, smiling. "Follow me."

And she seated them at a round table in the back. Edward greeted several customers.

When the waitress took their order, she kidded with Edward. Edward knows everyone in here, Violet thought.

The children and Grandfather were given special treatment by Rita and the waitress. After eating spaghetti and meatballs with heaps of homemade bread, they finished with coconut cream pie.

"In the morning," Edward promised, "you'll see my zoo. I know you'll like it."

"I know we will," Jessie said. "Is every animal your friend?"

"Every single one!" Edward said. "The town likes the animals, too. It's their taxes that helps me add new animals and build comfortable homes for them."

"I can see you're happy in your work," Grandfather said.

Edward nodded. "My zoo keeps me young, James."

Going to the zoo tomorrow would be exciting, Violet thought. She just hoped it was better kept than Edward's house!

CHAPTER 2

The Mix-Up

Benny, awakening before anyone else, climbed down the bunk's ladder and tiptoed to the closet. He pulled on pants and a shirt. Then he sat by the window to wait until Henry woke up.

After a few minutes, unable to wait any longer, he went over to Henry and whispered, "Henry, Henry, are you awake?"

Groaning softly, Henry rolled over and opened his eyes. "I am now," he said.

"Get ready. We're going to the zoo," Benny urged.

Sitting up, Henry said. "Look at you, Benny. You're dressed and ready to go."

Benny nodded.

"Okay," Henry said, swinging his legs over and rubbing his eyes. "I'll bet we're the first ones at the breakfast table."

But he was wrong. Coming into the kitchen, he was surprised to see Violet setting the table and Jessie mixing pancakes. Henry pitched in and broiled bacon while Benny poured orange juice.

Edward and Grandfather soon joined them. Edward's bushy eyebrows shot up. "Well, well, what have we here?" he said. "What a treat." He chuckled. "I only keep a few groceries on hand, but I see you've found a use for them."

"Edward," Jessie began as she set a stack of pancakes on the table, "I wonder if . . ."

"Yes?" he looked at her expectantly, pulling a chair to the table and sitting down.

"All of us like to cook and clean and garden." Jessie paused, passing the syrup. "And, well, we'd like to do a few things for you."

Edward chewed his bacon. "That would be wonderful. An old bachelor like me doesn't pay much attention to the house. Or have many home-cooked meals."

"Could we stack up your newspapers and magazines?" Violet asked.

"Of course." Edward thoughtfully rubbed his chin. "You know, there's an old cabinet in the basement. Maybe you could bring it up and hide them in there. Anything else you find down there that might be useful," he added, "haul it up."

"Thanks," Henry said. "If you like, we could plant a few shrubs and flowers, too."

"I'd like to have a hand in that, too," Grandfather said.

"Great!" Edward said, smiling. "I've got plenty of cash in that cookie jar." He pointed to an orange glass pumpkin with a green stem for the lid. "Help yourselves to whatever you need to buy."

"Thank you!" Benny said eagerly. "We won't waste it. I'll help weed and plant flowers."

Edward threw back his head and laughed.

"I can see your visit is going to be the best thing that's happened around here for a long time." Then he patted his stomach. "That was delicious. Usually I eat a bowl of dry cereal." He rose. "And now, are you ready for your tour of the zoo?"

"I'm ready!" Benny said promptly, jumping up from the table.

"I think we all are," Grandfather Alden said. "Lead the way, Edward."

And so on a beautiful morning with the sun streaming through the leaves, they walked to Marlow's Zoo.

Going through the iron-grilled gates, they walked down a tree-lined path. Birds sang and tigers rumbled.

A young woman carrying a bucket walked toward them. She wore khaki knee-length shorts and a matching shirt.

Edward waved. "Pat!" he shouted. "Come meet my friends."

She hurried over. "Hi," she said. "This must be the Alden family." A smile lit her tanned face. "Edward's been talking about your visit for weeks."

"This is Pat Kramer," Edward said, introducing each of the Aldens. "Pat's the best animal keeper this side of the St. Louis Zoo. I don't know what I'd do without her."

Pat shook James Alden's hand and then each of the children's. "If I can explain anything about the animals, let me know," she offered pleasantly.

"Thanks," Benny said.

"And that goes for all of us," Henry added.

Pat smiled. "I have to get back to Leona."

"Leona?" Violet questioned.

"Leona, the lion," Pat said. "She hasn't been herself lately, so I'm giving her a special diet."

"Let me know how she reacts," Edward said.

"I will," she promised and went on her way.

Looking over the zoo, the Aldens could see that many animals were not in cages.

"I think it's wonderful that many of the animals aren't behind bars," Jessie said.

Edward, strolling along, said, "Each animal has an area that is as close to its home in the wild as we can make it." He stopped before three giraffes. "In some cases a moat separates visitors from the animals," Edward explained, pointing to a deep ditch between them and the long-necked giraffes, who munched contentedly on tree leaves. Once they stopped to stare at their visitors, their soft eyes with long lashes blinking at the Aldens.

"Wow! Look how tall they are," Benny said, leaning back and looking down. "They have a longer neck than Miss Harrington, my first-grade teacher."

Violet read the sign. " 'Grizzly Bear.' " Puzzled, she glanced at Edward. "Grizzly bear?" she repeated.

Edward bent over to read the sign for himself. "Grizzly Bear!" He shook his head. "Well, now, we can see *that's* not right."

"Let's see what it says by the elephants," Benny shouted, running ahead.

He read the square card in front of the four adult elephants and one baby. "This sign says 'Monkeys'!" Placing his hands on his hips, he said, "Did I read it wrong?"

"No," Violet said. "You're right, the card is wrong."

"Well, I'll be," Edward said, catching up. Bewildered, he hurried to the Bird House. "Look at this," he said to the others who followed.

Jessie peered at the sign. "Why, the birds are all labeled 'Panthers,' 'Lions,' and 'Tigers.' " As if in protest, the birds shrilled and screeched.

Outside the Bird House, Benny passed a desertlike area on which a black snake slithered over the sand. "This card says 'Fox,' " Benny said.

Jessie, Violet, and Henry laughed. "Someone is playing a funny prank on Edward."

But Edward didn't laugh. "What's going on?" he asked. "This is an awful mix-up!"

Grandfather stepped forward, a smile twitching at the corners of his mouth. "It's a joke, Edward. Don't worry."

"Well," Edward growled. "I don't find it very funny."

"We'll put the signs in their right places," Violet said, snatching up the FOX sign.

Soon all of them had been returned.

"Good, good," Edward murmured. "I hope there are no more pranks!"

On the way home, Jessie glanced at Edward and could see he was still upset. "How about a nice dinner at home?" she asked. "We'll cook your favorite."

Edward's smile wiped away his gloom. "I like a good steak, baked potatoes, and tossed salad."

"That's easy," Henry said.

When they arrived at the house, Edward said, "But you'll need to go to the store. Mike's Grocery is only two blocks that way." Pointing in the opposite direction from the zoo, he dug in his pocket and pulled out some money, giving it to Jessie. "Now you can buy whatever you need."

Violet and Jessie, not wasting any time, hurried down the road.

Before long they were back and went directly to the kitchen.

Jessie stopped, her mouth dropping open. "Henry! Benny! You've cleaned the whole kitchen!"

Violet smiled. "Even the floor has been mopped."

"We wanted to surprise you," Benny said.

"You certainly did," Jessie said.

Henry unloaded the groceries while Violet made a salad and Jessie scrubbed six big potatoes and wrapped them in foil.

That evening everyone was seated at the dining room table. When the thick seared steaks and steaming potatoes were served, Edward's eyes lit up.

Cutting into his steak, Edward beamed. The children could see he felt a lot better than when he saw the mixed-up signs. They were glad they could cheer him up.

CHAPTER 3

The Snapshot

The next day the four Aldens walked to the store and bought lots of groceries to stock Edward's cupboards. They carried sack loads of apples, milk, bread, eggs, chicken, lettuce, tomatoes, onions, oranges, grapes, peas, green beans, orange juice, cereal, muffins, and hamburger meat.

When they arrived home, they carefully put the food away. Afterward they dusted every piece of furniture.

"You know Edward told us to bring up the cabinet from the basement," Violet said.

"Oh," Benny cried, clapping his hands. "Could we explore the basement?"

Henry chuckled. "I'm ready. Are you, Jessie?"

"I sure am," she said, heading toward the stairs.

First Henry went downstairs, followed by Jessie, then Violet, and finally Benny.

Boxes were stacked in corners, and a lamp as tall as Henry was in the center. Benny's eyes were wide as he peered at the many things strewn about. "Where should we start?" he asked.

Stepping over an old heater, Henry tipped over an empty box. "Anywhere you want to, Benny. Edward said we could bring upstairs anything we could use."

"Oh, boy," Benny said, going to a dark corner and kneeling down to open an old tin box. He picked up something small. "How pretty," he said, holding up an orange and black trinket.

"Look," Henry said, pointing to a wooden cabinet. "This must be what Edward mentioned." Opening the two doors, he peeked inside. "This will be just fine to store his magazines and newspapers."

Violet ran her hand over the dark wood. "I'll bet this is a hundred years old."

"Maybe it was his mother's sewing cabinet," Jessie said. "Edward told us he grew up in this house, so I know many of these things belonged to his parents."

"Let's carry this upstairs," Henry said. He lifted one end, and Violet and Jessie the other. They started up the steps.

They set the cabinet near Edward's chair in the living room.

"Did you notice that bookcase by the furnace?" Jessie asked.

"Perfect!" Violet exclaimed. "We could put some of Edward's books in there."

So they carried it upstairs. "What's this?" Jessie asked, picking up an album that was on the lower shelf.

Sitting down, Violet turned the pages of an old photo album. She peered closely at an old snapshot. "Look! This is Edward!"

Henry, looking over her shoulder, exclaimed, "Edward was a pilot in World War

Two. He was either in Japan or Germany. Those were the two main areas of fighting during the war."

"A pilot!" Violet said in surprise. "Who would have thought it? Edward is such a gentle man." She picked up the small photo. "This must be Edward in his pilot's suit, and, look, there's a pair of silver wings pinned to the collar of his leather jacket. And in the background is a plane with the words, 'The Wildcats.' "

Jessie took the picture and studied it. "Next to Edward is a real wildcat on a chain. Do you suppose that was their mascot?"

"I'm sure of it," Henry said. "I want to ask him about these things." He walked away. "Ouch!" he groaned, rubbing his shin. "I stumbled over this pile of books."

Jessie laughed. "It isn't a pile now. Books are scattered everywhere."

Henry studied the bookcase. "We could paint this and set it on the other side of Edward's big chair."

A noise in back of her caused Jessie to turn around. Suddenly her mouth formed an O of astonishment. "Oh, no!" she whispered. "Benny, what have you done?"

Benny stared down at his shirt. "I decorated myself," he said proudly.

"Oh," Violet said in a dismayed voice. "You certainly did." She touched one of the red and white hooks. "You got into Edward's fishing tackle box."

Benny touched one of the fishhooks that he'd pinned on his shirt. Dozens of different-colored feathered fishhooks covered his shirt. Henry tried to get one off, but the hook was embedded in the cloth.

"It's a good thing that's an old T-shirt," Jessie said quietly. "We'll have to cut off every hook!"

Benny asked, "Did I do something wrong?"

Violet said, "Fishhooks are hard to get loose. And," she added in a firm tone, "they're dangerous and shouldn't be played with."

"I won't do it again," Benny promised.

"I know you won't," Violet said.

Jessie, with great care, cut off every fish-hook. Benny's shirt was filled with holes. "What can I do with it now?" he asked.

"Don't worry about it, Benny," Henry said. "You can use it to help us polish this cabinet."

So they all pitched in and rubbed the wood to a beautiful sheen, then placed the antique cabinet by Edward's chair.

"What a nice addition to the living room," Jessie said, standing back.

"Yes, isn't it?" Violet agreed, placing on top of it a blue vase she'd found.

When they finished, the children prepared a delicious dinner.

Edward's eyebrows lifted when he saw the shiny glasses, and two candles in the center of the round table. "I didn't know my house could look so beautiful!" Edward said. He smiled when the meal was served. Baked chicken, peas, mashed potatoes, muffins, and for dessert, hot apple pie topped with ice cream.

"My grandchildren are very competent," Grandfather said proudly.

That night everyone slept well. The children were tired from their busy day.

The following morning Henry said, "I noticed a bookstore across the street from Mike's Grocery. Shall we see what's in it?"

"Oh, let's," Jessie said eagerly.

"Aren't we going to the zoo?" Benny asked in a disappointed voice.

"Of course, we are," Violet answered. "First the bookstore, then the zoo."

Entering the bookstore, the children were greeted by a tall lanky man who was bald and wore glasses. "Come in," he said in a welcoming voice. He bent down and asked Benny, "And what kind of books do you like to read?"

"Books about animals," Benny said quickly.

"Ahh," the skinny man said, raising his brows and glancing at the older children.

Jessie laughed. "Yes, we're all interested in animals."

"Especially animals in a zoo," Henry said.

"I see." The man rubbed his chin.

"You see," Violet continued, "we're visiting Edward Marlow who owns the zoo.

We'll be spending lots of time with the animals."

"Oh." A strange expression crossed the man's thin face, but it quickly passed, and he poked his glasses up on his long nose.

"Well, I'll find you all kinds of animal books," he said. "By the way, I'm Mac Thatcher, the owner of the shop."

"I'm Henry Alden," Henry said, placing a hand on Benny's shoulder, "and this is my little brother, Benny, and my two sisters, Violet and Jessie."

"Pleased to meet you," Mac Thatcher said, tilting his head and studying each one. Then he handed Benny a book. "This is a good book on zoo animals and what they eat." He gave another book to Violet. "This tells how they're captured and brought to zoos, and this one," he said, handing a book to Jessie, "is about baby animals in the zoo."

"This is great!" Benny said, flipping through the pictures of camels, rhinoceroses, elephants, lions, seals, bright-colored birds, and monkeys.

Mac Thatcher piled up books faster than

the children could look at them, and he told them about each different kind of animal. There were books on jungle animals, on all sorts of monkeys, one on the African lion, another on the Bengal tiger. There were books on gorillas, bears, and hippopotamuses.

"Stop," Violet begged. "I can't keep track of all the books you're showing us."

"Mr. Thatcher, you certainly know a lot about animals," Benny said admiringly.

"Call me Mac," he said in a kind voice. "Yes, I know my animals."

"Do you spend a lot of time at the zoo?" Benny asked.

But Mac didn't answer. He wheeled about and reached for another book.

"Do you spend a lot of time at the zoo?" Violet asked again, thinking he hadn't heard Benny.

Mac stared at her but pressed his lips together, not responding.

CHAPTER 4

More Trouble at the Zoo

When the children arrived home from the bookstore, they greeted Grandfather, who was digging holes for the new shrubs he had bought that morning.

Entering the house, they were surprised to see Edward in an angry conversation with a woman in a red suit and a black hat.

Edward stopped talking when he saw the children. "Hi, kids," he called. He briefly introduced them to the woman, whose name was Helen Brooks. She scarcely gave them a glance as she impatiently tapped her shoe.

After saying hello to her, the Aldens excused themselves and went into the kitchen.

They sat around the table while Jessie poured milk into three glasses and one pink cup, which was Benny's.

As they drank, they couldn't help overhearing Edward arguing with Helen Brooks.

"I tell you," Miss Brooks said in a stern voice, "that zoo of yours is not worth another penny of the taxpayers' money!"

Edward shot back a cold reply, "The zoo means everything to the children in Rosedale, and to lots of adults, too."

Helen Brooks sneered. "That's the most ridiculous thing I've ever heard. The zoo should be closed down. It costs thousands of dollars a year for food and medicine alone!" She continued in a raspy voice, "As a member of the town council, I intend to bring this up at the next meeting!"

"And what will happen to the monkeys and lions and all the other animals?" Edward shouted.

"How should I know?" Helen Brooks snapped back.

"If you had a heart, you'd care," Edward said sadly.

"Animals can be sent to other zoos," Helen said in a quarrelsome tone, "or you can give them away. I don't care!"

"I'll never give my animals away," Edward answered defiantly. "Each one means a lot to me!"

"That's too bad!" Helen said. "At the next meeting the zoo will be the first order of business!"

The children had stopped drinking and stared at one another. Violet felt a stab of concern. The town council couldn't get rid of Edward's zoo, she thought, and all his wonderful animals. Or could they? Jessie and Henry had the same thought.

Benny pushed his milk away. "I think the zoo is great," he murmured. He looked as if he were going to cry.

Henry jumped up. "I'll tell that Helen Brooks how *we* feel about the zoo," he said in a low voice.

"No," Jessie whispered. "Let's wait and see what Edward wants us to do."

Slowly, Henry sank back. "I guess you're right. But that woman . . ."

"I know," Violet said.

"You can be certain that I'll be at the next council meeting!" Edward shouted. "You won't get away with this!"

"You're stubborn, Edward Marlow!" Helen retorted, "but it won't do you any good!"

The door slammed and it was quiet.

For a moment all the Aldens heard was the tick of the clock. Then Benny stood up and rushed into the living room. "We heard what that mean woman said!" he cried. "The zoo won't be shut down, will it?"

Jessie, Violet, and Henry stood in the doorway, waiting for Edward's answer.

Edward shook his head. "Not if I can help it!" He glanced at each one. "Hey! Don't look so glum! I have lots of people on my side."

Benny smiled.

So did Jessie. But she wondered if Edward had any friends on the town council.

"Let's go check out the animals at the zoo!" Edward said.

As they walked along, Henry began, "Edward, we found a picture of you in a pilot's uniform." He looked at Edward, uncertain if he was intruding or not.

Surprised, Edward smiled. "Oh, you found the one of me and our squadron's mascot, Billy. That was when I was in the air force in Texas."

"Billy looked fierce," Violet said.

"He *was* fierce!" Edward said. "He was one of the fiercest wildcats I've ever seen. When I saw him, he was in a tiny cage and I was determined to put him in an area where he could run. I found an unused dog run and rented it. There Billy could prance, sleep in the sun, or just play with the leaves."

"Billy must have been special," Jessie said, noticing Edward's caring face.

"He was!" Edward said emphatically. "After the war was over and I returned from overseas, I went back to Texas for Billy. Other soldiers had taken care of him. At first I didn't know what I'd do, but Billy gave me the idea of raising money for a zoo, a place where animals could have freedom to roam about. I've always loved animals, and this gave me a purpose in life." He paused, re-membering. "Billy was my first zoo inhabi-tant."

"What happened to Billy?" Benny asked.

"My wildcat lived to a ripe old age, then died in his sleep."

Entering the zoo's gates, Benny was ex-cited to see the animals.

The children strolled by the elephants where a boy about Henry's age was grooming a baby elephant. When he saw Edward, he stopped and waved.

"Hi, David," Edward called. "He looks good!"

"Thanks," the boy said.

"That's David Adams," Edward ex-plained, moving on to the monkeys' area. "He's a reliable helper after school and on Saturdays. During the summer, he works three days a week. You'll have to get to know him."

They stopped to watch the monkeys. Sev-eral flew through the air on a trapeze while others played in the trees, swinging from branch to branch.

"Isn't that one cute?" Violet said, pointing at the smallest monkey. His bright button eyes peeked at them through a cluster of leaves.

Edward chuckled. "You know zoos often name their animals, and I enjoy naming mine. That's Amos, a real show-off. He loves people and is a smart little fellow."

Amos swung down and plucked a tin cup off the ground and hugged it to his chest.

"I'll bet that's his very own cup," Benny said. "Just like I have my pink cup."

"He's an imp. But everyone loves him," Edward said. "He likes to clown for an audience, and when they clap, he claps back."

Edward moved on.

"I like Amos," Benny said, following the others. He glanced back for one last glimpse of the monkey.

At the zebra enclosure, Violet said, "The zebras' coloring is so different."

"Good camouflage on the plains," Edward answered.

"How striking! White stripes on black," Jessie said.

"Oh?" Henry teased. "I thought it was black stripes on white."

Puzzled, Benny asked, "Which is it?"

"Whatever you want it to be," Violet said, smiling.

A roar startled them. They hurried around the corner and saw two orange-and-black-striped tiger cubs rolling about in the dirt. Nearby, the mother swam in the pool.

"I didn't know cats liked water," Jessie said.

"Not many of them do," Edward explained, "but the Bengal tiger from India is the exception. Isn't Zelda a beauty?"

"Zelda's jaws are huge!" Violet said.

"Zelda eats about ten pounds of meat a day and a beef shank every Wednesday," Edward said. As if knowing she were being talked about, Zelda opened her mouth and roared. Edward chuckled. "Zelda knows it's almost dinnertime."

The two cubs, biting and growling, continued to roll about in play.

"Oh, here's a sight you'll like to see," Edward said, crossing to the other side.

Two bears splashed in a pool, shoving a log back and forth. "You need to give the animals playthings," Edward said. "Otherwise they get bored. It gives them good exercise, too."

"The way they toss that log," Jessie said, "you'd think it was as light as a toothpick."

"Brown bears are strong, all right," Edward said, walking on to the giraffes.

Suddenly, Pat caught up with them. "The electricity is off in the kitchen," she said breathlessly.

"What!" Edward whirled about. "I'll check the transformers."

"I've already done that," Pat said. "All of them are in place. I phoned the electrician and he'll be here as soon as he can."

Edward frowned. "Why is the electricity off?" He gave Pat a worried glance. "Without electricity, the big food processor will be off. It will take hours to mash the food and chop vegetables. And there'll be no hot water to mix with the food," Edward said, running his fingers through his gray hair. "Do you kids want to help?"

"You bet!" Benny answered.

"Come with me to the kitchen. We'll have to slice vegetables, fruit, meat, and get the bales of hay for the elephants," Edward said.

Violet hurried after Edward. She frowned, deep in thought. First the animals' signs were switched. Then Helen Brooks wanted to close down the zoo. Now the kitchen electricity was cut off. She didn't like it. She didn't like it at all.

CHAPTER 5

Hungry Animals

The children chopped and cut fruits and vegetables until their fingers were stiff. They sliced bananas, carrots, oranges, and apples.

Pat took out the meat from the huge refrigerator and hurriedly sliced the meat for the big cats. She worked fast and well. In the background they could hear growls, roars, squalls, screeches, whistling, and squeaking. Pat glanced over at Violet. "You can certainly tell the animals are hungry," she said.

"All these different dinners you need to prepare," Jessie said in amazement. "I didn't know there was so much work in running a zoo." She threw three oranges in a bowl, which already contained a half pound of carrots, a half pound of cabbage, and five apples. This was one bear's diet.

Pat stopped what she was doing to come to Jessie's side and add a pound of beef mix and drizzle honey over the entire meal.

Jessie started on the second bear's dinner. This wasn't as hard since she'd already done one. At least nothing needed chopping.

Pat, slicing off large chunks of fat from the beef, chuckled. "You'd be surprised how many diets we've tried. Lions, though, are particular, like your ordinary house cat. Finicky. If they don't like the food you give them, the lions simply give a swish of their tails and leave it. Sometimes it takes months to get the right balance that will tempt them." Pat's soft blue eyes sparkled. She liked to talk about her work. "We mix nutritious food with beef, but if I mix in too much of the nutritious food, the cat won't eat it. It's hard to find just the right healthy combination." As she spoke, she cut meat off a joint of beef. "I miss the large electric knives that we usually work with."

"The lions should like that," Jessie said, eyeing the huge chunks of meat.

"Oh, they will," Pat said.

"Do the animals get fed only once a day?" Violet asked, rinsing off fish for the seals.

"No," Pat replied, scooping back a wisp of hair. "Usually they eat once in the morning, have an afternoon snack, and dinner at night. We need to chop food for the special diets. Often the animals won't eat the food if it isn't in bite-sized pieces. Then, too, when we cut up the food it's easier to add the vitamins and supplements that the animals need."

Edward rushed into the kitchen. "The electrician arrived, so you can use the appliances," he said.

"What was wrong?" Pat asked.

"Someone cut a few wires!" Edward replied bitterly.

"Oh, no," Pat exclaimed. "What a rotten

thing to do! Why would they do it?"

"That's a good question," Edward replied. "Something's going on here and I don't like it!"

Pat shivered. "I don't either."

"We'll need to be more watchful," Edward said, plucking a piece of straw from his denim shirt.

"Looks like you've fed the elephants," Pat said.

"Yes," Edward answered. "David returned just in time to help me." He sighed. "Good thing my zoo is small or we'd be here until midnight."

David hurried in. "It's scary about the cut wires," he said anxiously. "I'd like to catch the one who did it!" He glanced at Pat. "What can I do?"

"Give the bears their food. They must be starved," Pat said.

David grabbed two large buckets, smiling at the Aldens. "Hi," he said. "Welcome to the zoo!"

"Let me help you." Jessie acted quickly, opening the door for him.

Edward introduced all the children to David.

"I'll be back in a minute for the seals' food," the boy called over his shoulder. He ran to the bears.

He returned in a few minutes and grabbed a bucket of fish. "The bears were hungry!" he said, running out again to feed the seals.

The calls and screams had gradually died down as the animals received their food.

Happy they could be of help, the Aldens walked home with Edward.

"I'm taking everyone to Rita's Restaurant tonight," Edward said. "You really saved the day."

"Isn't it strange that someone cut the wires," Henry said. "It caused a lot of work."

"I know," Edward said grimly, his face tired with lines. "I'll find out who did it, though."

Jessie gave him a sharp look. Was there some person Edward suspected? Was it the same person who'd switched the animals' tags? Who could it be? Pat certainly knew all about the zoo. It would be easy for her.

But she was so nice. Was it Helen Brooks? She wanted to get rid of the zoo. Would she really stoop to such mean tricks? Jessie plucked a leaf from a tree and tore it into little pieces. She didn't know what to think.

Arriving home, they told Grandfather that Edward wanted to take them to Rita's for supper. He was delighted, and after everyone had cleaned up, they left together.

Over a bowl of tomato soup, Henry told Grandfather what had happened.

"Did someone deliberately snip the wires, Edward?" Grandfather asked, his eyebrows raising up a bit.

Edward nodded. "I'm positive, but, of course, I don't know who."

The waitress cleared the table and brought sandwiches stacked with slices of ham and swiss cheese.

The meal ended with strawberry sundaes for everyone.

The next morning the children rose early and fixed cereal with bananas and toast, plus their usual orange juice and milk.

Violet and Jessie watered the flowers while Benny helped Henry paint Edward's bookcase. All morning they worked, then they packed a picnic lunch in a cooler and walked to the city park.

The park's green grass and blue pond shimmered in the sunlight. Large trees shaded picnic tables and the swings.

"Could I have a ride on the swings?" Benny asked.

"Sure, come on," Henry said, smiling. "I'll push you so high you'll touch the sky."

In a short time, Henry left Benny to swing alone and chinned himself on the iron bar. When he'd finished, Jessie chinned herself just as many times as her brother.

Benny had moved to the jungle gym and climbed all over it. Violet tried out the rings. Holding her arms straight, she did a handstand, then flipped over to the ground.

From atop the jungle gym, Benny clapped. "That was great, Violet." He began to climb down. "I'm hungry."

"I think we should eat our lunch over there," Violet said, pointing to a picnic table surrounded by oaks and at the edge of the pool.

"Perfect!" said Jessie. "It's shady and by the water."

They hurried over and Henry set the table. Jessie took out the tuna salad sandwiches and potato chips.

Violet poured milk from the thermos while Benny sat waiting, eager to begin.

They enjoyed the beautiful day, the blue sky with white fleecy clouds, and the soft breeze.

Benny was sad to leave, but Jessie promised they'd come back. But first, she thought, we have to solve the mystery at the zoo!

CHAPTER 6

Snoopy Miss Brooks

On Saturday afternoon the children walked to the zoo. Everything seemed to be going smoothly since the electricity had been restored in the kitchen. Even Edward was in a good humor.

It was a cloudy day, but it didn't dampen the children's spirits. And then, too, the new T-shirts Edward had given them cheered them up. Edward had asked the Aldens to each choose one they liked from the zoo's gift shop. Today they all wore jeans and their new T-shirts, on the back of which, in large letters, was the name, MARLOW'S ZOO. The front of each T-shirt was very different. Violet's lavender T-shirt had a black panther painted on the front. Benny wore a white T-shirt with a monkey swinging from a tree. Jessie's red T-shirt carried a sketch of seals, one diving in the water and another sunning itself on a rock. Henry's black T-shirt had a striking head of a zebra. Even Grandfather had gotten one. His was blue with a golden lion.

The children walked along, Henry and Violet behind Benny and Jessie. Benny and Jessie picked up speed when the gates of the zoo came into view.

All at once Benny's footsteps slowed.

"What's the matter, Benny?" Violet asked softly.

"That black car parked at the curb," he murmured, dragging his feet, not wanting to go by.

"It's okay," Jessie said, noticing the woman seated behind the wheel. "It's Helen Brooks. Just say hello and pass on by."

The car windows were rolled down, and

Jessie politely greeted Miss Brooks, as did the others.

Benny gave her a timid hello.

"Children!" Miss Brooks ordered, a frown remaining on her pointed face, "Come here!" She leaned across the seat.

Stiffly Henry moved to the car, wondering what she wanted.

"Has there been trouble at the zoo?" she asked, her dark eyes studying Henry's face.

"Mr. Marlow could answer that," Henry said. He didn't want to lie, but he didn't want to give her information that would damage the zoo.

"Well," Helen Brooks grumbled, "I don't live too far from here, and the other night the animals were making a dreadful racket. I know *something* disturbed them, and I want to know what."

Jessie, who had joined Henry, peered inside the car. "The animals are often restless and noisy at night," she answered, neatly sidestepping Miss Brooks' question.

Helen Brooks' mouth turned down in a sour line. "I can see I won't gain information from the four of you! You're Edward's friends, and that's that!"

Violet silently agreed. She had no intention of telling her about the problem with the food.

Helen Brooks straightened up behind the steering wheel, glaring. "Run along, children." She picked up a notebook, jotting down a few words.

"Why do you suppose she's sitting by the zoo?" Violet questioned as they moved away.

"I don't know what she's looking for," Jessie said. "Maybe she's counting the number of people who visit the zoo."

"You mean if not enough people come she'll say the zoo should be closed?" Benny asked, his eyes big and questioning.

"That's one possibility," Henry answered, as he chuckled. "But here's four she can count!" And they passed through the zoo's gates.

"I think Helen Brooks is a snoop!" Benny said indignantly.

"It does look like she's spying," Jessie said. "I'd like to get hold of her notebook."

"We'll tell Edward about her," Violet promised.

Their first stop was at the tropical Bird House where heat and moisture filled the air. The beautiful colored birds screeched and flew about. Parrots from South America had vivid colors . . . green, blue, and yellow.

Benny liked the laughing kookaburra from Australia with its flat bill, while Violet preferred the long-legged pink flamingos.

They soon left, and Jessie noticed Pat at the seal pond. They hurried over to see why the seals were clapping their flippers.

"Hi, kids," Pat called cheerfully, bending over a bucket of fish. "Watch this!" She tossed a fish in the pond, and a seal, eager for a tasty snack, dived after it. Coming up with the trout in his mouth, the seal swam to the edge and clambered up on a rock where he perched and clapped for more.

"That's all there is," Pat said, tipping over the bucket. "Until tonight."

Pat turned back to the Aldens. "It's good to see you again," she said, smiling. "I believe you like this zoo as much as I do."

"Oh, we do!" Benny piped up. "The zoo is great!"

Pat chuckled and leaned over the railing overlooking the honking seals. "If Edward ever wants to sell this place, I'd be ready to buy it."

Violet shot Henry a surprised look. Maybe, she thought, Pat was the guilty one. Did she think that if she could do enough mischief in the zoo she might be able to buy it at a good price?

"Let's go and see Amos the monkey," Benny said. "He misses me."

Henry laughed. "How do you know, Benny? Have you two been having secret conversations?"

Benny grinned. "In a way."

"It's easy to get attached to particular animals," Pat said. "And you'd be surprised how attached animals get to their keepers. Some animals want only Edward to feed them and are upset when they see me coming with their food." She paused. "It's too bad, though, when visitors feed them, unless it's the prepared food sacks that the zoo sells."

"Do people often feed them the wrong things?" Violet wanted to know.

"Yes. They feed them everything." She shook her head. "One man held out a jar of olives to the elephant. He thought the elephant would just take one, but to his shocked surprise, the elephant swallowed the whole jar."

"Oh, no," Jessie said. "Was the elephant all right?"

"I kept the elephant under observation for a week, and after that time, I knew he was okay." She walked toward the Bengal tigers' area. "See you later," she said with a pleasant wave.

Jessie watched as Pat walked away. She liked Pat a lot, but ever since her remark about wanting to buy the zoo, she'd begun to doubt her.

Benny ran ahead to see Amos, who immediately showed off by putting his tin cup on his head.

Violet read the sign. " *'These monkeys are capuchins, one of the most intelligent breed of monkeys. They are always eager to learn.'* "

Benny nodded as if he'd known this all along. "Could we go to the bookstore and find another book on monkeys?" he asked.

"Good idea," Henry replied. "We'll go right now."

They left the zoo and were soon in the bookstore searching for books on monkeys.

Mac Thatcher, sitting on a high stool by the cash register, stood up. "What can I do for you today?" he questioned.

"I need a book on monkeys," Benny said.

"Hmmm," Mac said, reaching for a book. "Here you go."

Benny opened the book but he was disappointed in the long words, fine print, and lack of pictures. "No, I want one for me," he said.

"Oh, a baby book," Mac said, carelessly giving him a book.

"Not a *baby* book!" Benny said, sticking out his chin. "I'm six years old!"

"All the monkey books are in that section," Mac said, pointing.

Benny soon lost himself hunting for just the right book.

"So what's going on at the zoo?" Mac asked, narrowing his eyes.

"Someone switched the animals' tags," Henry answered.

"Oh, that's too bad," Mac said, but he didn't look very sorry. "Anything else?"

"The electricity was cut off," Jessie said.

"Oh?" Mac said, his eyes lighting up with interest. "What happened?"

"We helped feed the animals until the electrician could get there," Jessie said.

"Well, well," Mac commented. Just then a small dog scampered over to Mac and began to whine and paw at his trouser leg. "What do you want, Scamper?" Mac asked.

Jessie glanced about, noticing the dog's food bowl under one of the shelves. It was empty. So was the water bowl.

"I think Scamper's hungry," Jessie said.

Mac shrugged. "Oh, I suppose he is. I forgot to feed him today."

Scamper lay down on an old rug, his bright eyes eagerly watching his master for a sign of food.

"If you tell me where you keep your dog's

food, I'll be glad to fill his bowl," Violet offered shyly.

"Forget it," Mac said. With a sigh, he went into the back room, and returned with Scamper's dinner.

"Satisfied?" Mac said with a scowl, glaring at the children.

"And water?" Jessie asked.

Mac grabbed the dog's bowl and filled it.

No one said anything as they observed the dog, eagerly eating and drinking. The bowls were soon empty.

After a few minutes, Benny shouted triumphantly, "I've found my book!"

Jessie and Violet looked over Benny's shoulders at the beautifully illustrated book on monkeys.

Henry paid for the book and they left, glad to leave gloomy Mac to himself.

"Mac Thatcher isn't nice to his dog," Benny pronounced, his mouth drooping.

"No. Mac Thatcher doesn't seem to care if he feeds Scamper or not," Jessie said. "He wasn't helpful in finding Benny's book either."

"He's an unhappy man," Violet said softly.

When they opened the front door, they saw Grandfather and Edward sitting at a small table. They were playing chess.

"Hi, Aldens," Edward called. "Is everything all right at the zoo?"

"Fine," Henry answered. "We saw Pat, then watched the monkeys for a while."

"But we did see Helen Brooks sitting in her car by the zoo," Jessie said.

"She asked us questions, but we didn't tell her a thing!" Benny said in a firm voice.

"Good for you!" Edward said.

"Then I got this book at the bookstore," Benny said, holding it out to Grandfather.

Grandfather paged through the book. "It's a wonderful book, Benny. I know you'll enjoy it!"

That was one of the many things Jessie liked about Grandfather. He always encouraged them to read, and often gave them books for presents.

"Whew! I'm hot!" Benny gasped, dropping onto the sofa.

"How about a cold glass of lemonade?" Jessie asked.

"You bet," he said, sitting up.

"And how about you, Edward and Grandfather?"

"That sounds good," Grandfather said.

Edward was concentrating so hard on the chess game he only nodded.

Even the night didn't bring any relief from the heat. It was very hot, even for late August.

Early the next morning the phone shrilled throughout the small house. The children were on their way downstairs.

Edward, dressed and ready to go out the door, said, "It's Pat at the zoo. She wants me to meet her at the seals. Something is wrong."

"Could we come along?" Henry asked.

Edward nodded. "Maybe you can help again. I can depend on you Aldens!" he said, pleased. "Your grandfather is still sleeping."

When they reached the seals, Pat was pouring water over a coughing seal, who con-

stantly clapped his flippers. Another seal lay
on the rocks, too still and quiet.

Edward stood before the seal pond, too
stunned to move. The pond had been
drained. It had been a hot night, and the seals
had been without water.

"Who could have done this?" Pat cried,
shaking her head. "It's good I was here early
this morning. I turned the water on, but it
will take a little while for the pool to fill.
Pat's face was pale and she looked helplessly
at the children.

Furious, Edward whirled and got some
buckets. Then he and the Aldens brought
buckets of water and doused the seals, who
clapped for more. The seal lying down
perked up at the first bucketful of water.

Once the pool was full and the seals were
again in the water, the children sat down to
rest. It was good to listen to the seals honking
and splashing with pleasure.

"This is terrible," Jessie said. "The poor
seals could have died."

"We'd better find out who's doing this,"
Henry said, "before Helen Brooks finds out.

The seals would fill a page in her notebook."

Violet said thoughtfully, "I wonder why Pat came to the zoo early today."

"I think it's Mac Thatcher!" Benny stated, his brown eyes flashing. "He hates animals, and that's why he's doing all these mean things."

"Whoa," Henry said. "Just because he forgot to feed his dog doesn't mean he's guilty."

"Then it's Helen Brooks," Jessie said with a firm nod. "If she could prove the animals were being mistreated, she could get the zoo closed in a minute."

Violet didn't answer. They didn't really have a clue, she thought, as to who the guilty person could be. And if they didn't find out soon, Edward would lose his zoo! Even worse, some animals might die.

CHAPTER 7

Too Hot, Too Cold

The next day was calm at the zoo. Maybe, Jessie thought, the strange things happening to the animals had stopped.

On the afternoon of the second peaceful day, Benny said, "Let's read our books."

"That would be fun," Violet said. "I'm almost finished reading the mystery I brought with me and I'm eager to see how it ends."

So they went outside and Henry spread out two blankets. There was only one tree in Edward's backyard, but it was a large apple tree and heavy with apples.

It was pleasant to enjoy the shade on such a warm day, to eat crisp apples, and to read.

At last they closed their books and folded their blankets. When they decided to visit the zoo, it was almost closing time.

Going through the gate, they found David. He was giving Joe, the elephant, a bath. "Hi, Aldens," he called with a smile, then returned to his work.

Joe patiently allowed David to use a brush to scrub him. Making wide soapy circles in the elephant's leathery hide, David soon covered Joe in white.

"Watch this," David said, chuckling and picking up a hose. "He loves his shower!" He sprayed the elephant, causing the soap to run down Joe's sides in white streams. Joe lifted his trunk and trumpeted his pleasure.

At last David coiled up the hose and came over to lean on the fence. "What did you do today?" he asked.

"Most of the day we read and ate apples," Benny said, grinning.

David nodded. "That sounds like a perfect

afternoon. Second only to working here with the animals."

"David," Henry asked, growing serious, "what do you think of what's been happening at the zoo?"

Frowning, David shook his head. "I wish I knew what was going on. If these awful things don't stop, I'm afraid Edward might lose the zoo." He paused. "I noticed Helen Brooks here again yesterday. She asked me a lot of questions, but I didn't give her any information that would hurt Edward."

"Good!" Jessie said. "I know she's waiting for a chance to find out something really damaging."

"I saw Pat talking to her," David said, "but I know she didn't give her any news, either."

I hope not, Jessie thought.

"Has anyone else been around asking questions?" Violet asked.

David shrugged. "Not that I noticed. I only work three days a week in the summer." He smiled. "I'd like to work with the animals every day. Someday," he announced, "I'm going to be a zookeeper."

"That would be a great job, David," Benny said. "Maybe I'll be one, too."

"We could work at the same zoo, Benny," David said, teasing. "Well," he sighed, "I'd like to stay and talk but I'd better get back to work. Pat wants me to check out the brown bears."

The Aldens strolled over to the leopards and watched a baby leopard playing with its mother.

Four chimes sounded. The zoo was closing. One boy, sitting on his father's shoulders watching the beavers, cried, "I don't want to leave."

"We'll come back, son," the father reassured him.

A man pushed a wheelchair before him. In the chair was an elderly woman with a lovely smile on her face.

Yes, Henry thought. Edward's zoo *had* to stay open. It gave so much enjoyment to so many different kinds of people.

In the morning the children planned to go to the zoo early. Edward was opening up that day and Pat was coming in later. They wanted their afternoon free, as Grandfather was taking them to a movie, then out for ice cream.

As soon as they entered the zoo's gates, they knew something was wrong. Going by the lions, they noticed how restless they were and how they paced back and forth, shaking their manes.

Hurriedly they followed Edward to the Bird House. "Let's see how our tropical friends are doing," Edward said, opening the door.

The macaw screeched, and the green parrot scolded, but on the whole the birds were unusually quiet. Many were hunched over and didn't move.

"Oh," Jessie cried, grabbing her arms, "it's cold in here!"

"I'm cold, too," Benny exclaimed.

"The heat's off!" Edward shouted, racing to the opposite wall and checking the thermometer. Immediately he turned up the heat, and when he faced them, an angry expression crossed his face.

"These birds could have died!" he said, his face red with fury. Helplessly he threw out his hands. "Let's check the others."

Sure enough, the brown bears from Alaska were slumped against the rocks, panting. The air-conditioning in their glassed-in area had been turned off.

Edward raced from one animal house to another, raising low temperatures and lowering high temperatures. The Aldens helped by bringing water to animals that were lying down, too uncomfortable to move.

At last all the animals had been checked, and when they were at ease again, the children relaxed, too.

"Maybe we should face Helen Brooks and ask her to leave the zoo alone!" Violet exclaimed.

"Not yet," Jessie cautioned. "If she isn't the one *doing* these things, she'd just love to hear about them."

"The best thing to do is keep our eyes open, and if we see anything suspicious, tell Edward," Henry advised.

"I hate to sit here and *wait* for things to happen," Violet said.

"It's the only thing we can do right now," Jessie admitted. "I don't like it any better than you do."

"Let's go home," Henry said. "We can't do any more here. Edward is in the Bird House and Pat will be coming soon."

As they left, a black car sped away.

"Who was that?" Benny said. "He was speeding!"

"Doesn't Helen Brooks have a black car?" Jessie asked.

"Yes," Violet responded quietly. "Was she spying again?"

Henry shook his head. "I don't think so. A man was behind the wheel."

Puzzled, they glanced at one another. The mystery was becoming deeper and deeper.

CHAPTER 8

Who Is Guilty?

In the afternoon the children went to the movies with Grandfather. And for a while they forgot about the zoo. But afterward, as they ate banana splits, Benny said, "Could we stop at the zoo on the way home, Grandfather?"

Surprised, Grandfather Alden said, "You spent all morning at the zoo."

"We want to see if the animals are all right," Jessie said. "When we left, Edward was still checking some of them that had suffered under the wrong temperature."

"Of course, we'll stop," Grandfather said with understanding. "I'm sure all the animals survived, but we can pick up Edward."

"Great!" Henry said. "Lately Edward looks so worn out from everything that's happened."

"It's a good thing we're here so we can help him," Violet said softly, finishing the last of her ice cream.

Mr. Alden studied his two granddaughters, proud of them. And how pretty they looked. Violet in her blue denim jacket and skirt, her hair tied with lavender ribbons, and Jessie in yellow flowered shorts and top.

He was proud of his grandsons, too. Handsome boys. Henry resembled him, tall and straight. Benny had an impish twinkle in his dark eyes.

Yes, he was a lucky man to have found his four loving grandchildren. To think that not too long ago they had hidden from him in an old boxcar, believing that he was a mean man who wanted to hurt them. If Violet hadn't become ill, he might never have found them. It was the doctor, a friend of his, who had led him to them. Yes, indeed, he was truly lucky. Never had he known children that were so ready to help, and not only him, but others as well.

Benny leaned forward. "Are we going, Grandfather?"

"Wh-what?" Grandfather stammered, coming back from his memories. "Oh, yes, yes." Smiling, he stood, paid the bill, and they left for the zoo.

They arrived at closing time as people were streaming out the front gates.

Jessie tugged at Henry's sleeve. "Isn't that Mac Thatcher from the bookstore?" she whispered, as a tall thin man went by.

Henry saw Thatcher walking down the sidewalk to a black car and unlocking it.

"That's him," Henry said firmly. "He doesn't look like the type who comes to the zoo for enjoyment!"

"There's the bad man from the bookstore," Benny shouted, pointing at the black car pulling away from the curb.

"That's him," Violet agreed. "What do you suppose he was doing here?"

"Maybe *he* was making the birds cold and the bears hot," Benny stated.

Thoughtfully, Jessie shook her head. "No, Benny, the temperature changes happened early this morning."

Pat Kramer hurried forward as the gates clanged shut. "I'm glad you're here," she said. Her usual smiling face was sober.

Alarmed, Violet stared at Pat. "Is something wrong?" she asked in a shaky voice.

"Yes," Pat said shortly. "Come with me and you can judge for yourself." She headed for Edward's office.

Without a word the children followed her. Grandfather, grim-faced, walked so fast that it was hard to keep up with him.

In the zoo office they were astonished to see Edward sitting slumped in his chair, his head in his hands.

"What is it?" Mr. Alden asked.

Edward lifted his head and opened a drawer in a file cabinet. It was empty. "Someone came into the office in plain daylight and stole all the animals' papers."

"How could that happen?" Henry asked.

"Pat and I were busy checking the animals. I didn't get to the office until late this afternoon." He sighed and ran his fingers through his hair. "The thief cleaned me out."

"What do the papers say?" Benny asked.

"Information about the animals," Edward answered. "Special diets are recorded, when they had their vaccinations, when they arrived at the zoo, and where they came from, facts I need to know."

Pat bit her underlip. "This is the worst prank yet!"

"I'd call it more than a prank!" Grandfather exclaimed. "It's vicious and damaging to the animals."

Edward shot his old friend a grateful glance. "You're right, James. I'll have to start over, recording all that information. I can remember a few things, but only a few."

"Between the two of us," Pat said, "we'll manage."

Papers were scattered on the floor, as if the robber had made a quick exit. The saddest sight, though, was the empty file drawers.

"Don't you think you should call the police now?" Henry asked.

Edward hesitated before replying. "I'd like to, but if I do, I know the zoo will close down. This is just the ammunition Helen Brooks is looking for!"

"Perhaps the police will be able to solve the case before Helen Brooks can find out," Jessie said, sitting down.

"Believe me, Jessie," Edward said, "I want to bring the thief to justice, but I can't risk having my zoo closed down."

That night the children had planned a special dinner, and they were glad they had. Edward needed something to take his mind off the animals.

As soon as they got home they began preparing meat loaf, broccoli with cheese, mashed potatoes, and apple salad, plus lemon cake for dessert.

As the meat loaf baked, the children fixed the rest of the dinner and discussed the case.

"We didn't see Helen Brooks today," Violet said. "Maybe she can't find enough information to bring before the town

council. Maybe she's given up."

"Don't we wish," Jessie said, chopping up the apples and celery. "But I think Helen Brooks is the kind of woman who, once an idea pops into her head, won't let go."

Benny agreed. "She never smiles. I know she's thinking of ways she can get rid of the animals!"

Henry peeled potatoes and dropped them into boiling water. He frowned. "Just because Helen Brooks doesn't smile doesn't mean she'd stoop to such low tricks to close the zoo."

Benny set the table in the dining room. Returning, he reported, "Edward and Grandfather are playing chess again."

"Good," Jessie said. "The game will take Edward's mind off his problems." She opened the oven and was pleased to see the meat loaf was nicely browned. Taking it out, she set it on a platter.

Violet stuck a fork in the boiling broccoli and decided it was cooked just enough. She put it in a bowl and poured the cheese sauce over it.

Henry put the mashed potatoes in a bowl while Benny poured the milk.

"I think," Jessie said, "that Mac Thatcher is acting very suspicious lately. We've seen him at the zoo, and he's curious about what's going on there. Why is he so interested?"

"You've got a point, Jessie," Henry said, dishing up the mashed potatoes. "Mac's a sourpuss all right, but he really hasn't any reason to put the zoo out of business."

"No," Jessie agreed, slicing the meat loaf. "He doesn't have as much reason as Pat. Remember what she said about buying the zoo?"

Violet placed the steaming broccoli on the table. "I really don't think Pat meant that." She shrugged her shoulders. "Wanting to buy the zoo was just a passing remark."

Henry sprinkled dressing over the apples and celery. "We all like Pat," he said, "but you can't deny that she's had the best opportunity to carry out everything that's taken place. After all, she works at the zoo."

Benny's mouth formed a big O. "So does David."

"I don't think it could be David," Violet said with a smile. "He's so sweet, and you can tell he truly loves the animals."

"Dinner is ready!" Jessie called.

Grandfather and Edward seated themselves at the table. Edward rubbed his hands together when he saw the wonderful dinner the children had prepared.

Jessie, sitting next to Grandfather, thought of the suspects. Each person they'd talked about had some reason to see the zoo shut down, but the Aldens didn't have any proof. Whoever the guilty one was, it seemed that he or she was going to get away with being cruel to innocent animals and maybe, closing a wonderful zoo.

CHAPTER 9

Where's Amos?

"That was a delicious dinner," Edward said, leaning back and patting his stomach.

"Are we going to finish our game of chess?" Grandfather asked.

Edward pushed back his chair. "Afraid not, James. I'm too tired, and I have to be wide awake to beat you! In fact," he said, rising and stretching, "I'm going to bed. I need to be at the zoo bright and early." He gave them all a half smile. "I don't know if I'll get much sleep, though."

Jessie glanced at Henry. It was too bad that Edward couldn't sleep because of worrying. If they could only do more to help.

They all went to bed shortly after Edward had turned in.

Violet, however, couldn't sleep. She gazed at the big yellow moon outside her window and hoped the animals were safe. She tossed and turned and hit her pillow. It wasn't fair that Edward, who was such a wonderful man, had to put up with trouble at his zoo.

At last Violet drifted off into a restless sleep. She dreamed a huge van hauled all the animals away. And when they visited the zoo, it was quiet and still. Not a bird whistled or a lion roared. Not one animal remained.

When Violet awakened, sunlight streamed in, and she heard voices from the kitchen. Leaping out of bed, she dressed and ran downstairs.

Jessie laughed, handing Violet a glass of orange juice. "Good morning, sleepyhead. You're just in time for breakfast."

Violet smiled. "I'm sorry I wasn't here to help." She was glad that she had only *dreamed* that the animals had disappeared.

After eating oatmeal and toast, the Aldens cleaned the kitchen, bought groceries at the store, and chatted with Grandfather, who was working in the yard.

"How do you like these red rosebushes I planted?" he asked.

"Beautiful," Violet said.

"Do you want us to do anything?" Henry asked.

"No," Grandfather answered. "I'm happy when I can dig in the dirt." He straightened, rubbing his back. "You run along to the zoo. I'm sure Edward needs you more than I do."

Suddenly, Violet stood on her tiptoes and kissed her grandfather. They were so lucky he loved them.

So the Aldens left for the zoo, hoping there would be no more trouble. Today they'd have fun looking around.

But when they saw Edward, he was standing by the seals with Pat, and both of them had grim faces.

"What now!" Jessie murmured.

"Hi, kids," Edward called, then turned

back and studied a list with Pat.

Violet's heart picked up a beat. Fearfully, she glanced around, but all the animals were in place and seemed happy and content.

"You two aren't smiling!" Benny said, not smiling himself. "Did another bad thing happen?"

"Yes, it did," Edward answered. "I went into the storeroom where we keep expensive animal food and diets." He shook his head. "Most of it is missing!"

"Oh, no," groaned Henry.

"Some animals," Pat explained, her forehead wrinkling, "have special diets, others need expensive vitamins, and it's all gone. Our storeroom was ransacked."

"What can we do?" Violet questioned.

"Do you suppose your grandfather would drive you over to Bridgeport and you could pick up a few items at the pet store? Pat and I have to stay here."

"We'd be glad to," Henry responded.

"There's no rush," Edward said. "Enjoy the zoo this morning, and this afternoon you can buy the food."

"Oh, good," Benny said. "I wanted to say hello to Amos!"

Pat smiled and handed the list of pet foods that were needed. "I don't know what we'd do without the Aldens," she said, squeezing Jessie's hand. Jessie smiled at Pat. Edward was lucky to have such a good worker. Then her smile faded. At least she *thought* he was. Surely Pat couldn't be the guilty one.

For the next hour they wandered around the zoo. They watched the seals as they dived and played in their pool.

"Remember the bad shape the seals were in when their pool was drained?" Violet said.

"Yes, they look much healthier today," Jessie said, pleased at their antics.

They moved on. The panther, sleek and black, sat and stared at them; the birds gave them a noisy greeting; and the elephants swished their tails and raised their trunks. The children laughed as they watched the animals, enjoying their playfulness.

"Could we go to the Monkey House now?" Benny coaxed.

"Yes, we've saved the best for last," Violet

said, walking toward the chattering monkeys.

A monkey swung by one arm from a branch, another carefully peeled a banana and ate it. They jumped from the trapeze to the trees, and it was hard to tell one from another.

Benny, his eyes following each one, tugged on his ear, puzzled. "Where's Amos? I know *exactly* what he looks like."

"He's probably hiding behind those rocks," Henry answered, chuckling. "Don't worry, he'll come out when he wants to."

Benny watched more closely. Amos's tin cup lay on the ground. "No," he said in a choked voice. "He isn't in there."

Jessie, Violet, and Henry joined Benny in trying to spot Amos. They knew how much Benny cared about him.

"Where could he be?" Benny asked.

"Maybe Pat took him out for an examination," Jessie said reassuringly.

Sadly, Benny shook his head. "No. Maybe someone has kidnapped him."

"We'll find out right now," Henry said.

They hurried out of the Monkey House. Henry spotted Edward by the Lion House.

"Edward," he called, running to meet him. "Is Amos being examined?"

Edward appeared startled. "Why, no. Isn't he in with the others?"

"We can't find him," Henry said. "Could he be hiding?"

Edward hurried over to the Monkey House and scanned each monkey. "He's not there," he said calmly. "We'll start a search, but there's no way he could have gotten free."

Benny's lowered lip trembled. "I knew it. Someone stole Amos. He'd never leave his tin cup behind unless he was snatched up before he could grab it." He reached in and grasped the cup and hugged it to his chest. Then he put it in his back pocket.

Jessie stared at the monkeys. If anything happened to Amos she knew how sad Benny would feel. Where could the poor little monkey be?

CHAPTER 10

Mac and the Monkey

On the way home from the zoo Henry tried to coax a smile out of Benny, but no matter what he did to cheer him, his little brother remained sad and silent.

"I'm sure Amos will turn up," Violet assured him. "He probably found a way to get out of the Monkey House, and he's hiding somewhere near."

Benny gazed at her with big brown eyes. "I-I hope so," he said in a shaky voice.

When they arrived home, Grandfather immediately noticed Benny's unhappy face.

"What's wrong?" he questioned, leaning over and lifting Benny's chin.

"E-Everything!" Benny stammered, fighting back tears. "Amos is gone!"

Grandfather looked inquiringly at Henry.

"Yes," Henry answered. "The monkey has vanished. But," he hastened to add, "I'm certain he'll turn up."

"Me, too," Jessie said. "I remember a story Pat told me about a zoo in California. There was this tiger who had lived in his enclosure for several years. Then one day a dynamite blast startled him, and before the unbelieving keepers' eyes, the tiger leapt over the moat as easily as if it didn't exist." She glanced at Benny to see if he was listening. "So you see, animals can escape from their homes if they want to."

Benny stared at Jessie. "What happened to the tiger?"

Smiling, Jessie said, "The zookeepers were able to capture him and put him back in his area. And he's living there to this very day."

"The tiger just got out by himself?" Benny asked, a glint of hope in his eyes.

"That's right," Jessie said, placing a comforting hand on Benny's shoulder.

"Maybe," he said in a hesitating voice, "Amos is waiting for Edward to put him back with his friends right now!"

"That's possible," Violet said, then turning to Grandfather, she asked, "Could you please drive us to Bridgeport?"

Grandfather raised his bushy brows. "Yes, but why?"

"Edward's storeroom was broken into, and valuable food and vitamins were stolen," Jessie explained. "Edward needs these things." She showed Grandfather the list of supplies.

"Of course I'll drive you," Grandfather said.

"First, we'll eat a little lunch, then we'll go," Violet said, going into the kitchen.

"I'm not hungry," Benny complained, but he followed her.

"*Not* hungry?" Henry exclaimed. "That's the first time I ever heard you say that, Benny."

"Could you eat just a little?" Violet urged, pouring milk.

Benny shook his head.

"Well," Grandfather said, pulling up a chair to the table, "after we buy pet food, we'll take it to Edward. And," he added, with a twinkle in his eye, "I'll bet Amos will be flying through the air on the trapeze."

Benny attempted a smile. "And I'll be holding out his tin cup to him."

Grandfather chuckled. "That's right."

"Now, can you eat a cup of chicken soup and a ham sandwich?" Jessie asked.

"I'll try," Benny said.

So after a good lunch, they cleaned up, and jumped into the station wagon.

Driving to Bridgeport, Benny was unusually quiet, but he wasn't as sad as before. When they arrived in town, Grandfather pulled into a space in front of the Bridgeport pet shop, and they all went in.

On a perch a green, yellow, and red parrot squawked, "Welcome! Come in!"

A clerk, waiting on a tall thin man, smiled at them and said, "I'll be with you in a moment."

Violet nudged Henry. "Isn't that Mac

Thatcher who the clerk is helping?"

Glancing at the man, Henry nodded. "I wonder what he's doing here," he said.

Mac turned his head. When he saw the Aldens, a frown darkened his face. "You're everywhere, aren't you?" he snarled.

The salesman, ignoring Mac's remark, ordered, "Please put the cage up on the counter, sir, so I can get a better look at the monkey."

"Monkey!" Benny burst out, whirling around to have a look. Much to Mac's displeasure, Benny peered inside the cage. The monkey began to chatter and hop about. "It's *him*!" Benny shouted.

"What are you babbling about?" Mac asked harshly, lifting the cage onto the counter. He glared at Benny. "Go away!"

"That's Amos from the zoo!" Benny gasped.

"Mind your own business!" Mac snapped. "Besides," he added, "how can you tell one monkey from another?"

The clerk studied the monkey from every angle. "I'll pay five hundred dollars for this

little fellow," he announced, opening the cash register.

"He's worth four times that!" Mac snarled.

"I know," the clerk said smugly, then lowered his voice, "but monkeys are on the endangered list. I shouldn't buy it at all, but I happen to have a buyer."

Benny pulled on Grandfather's sleeve. "Please! Stop Mac from selling Amos."

"We have no proof that that's Edward's monkey," Grandfather said kindly.

"Amos shouldn't be in such a little cage," Benny begged, looking from one person to another. "I know it's Amos." He thought for a minute. "Wait, I'll show you." He reached in his back pocket and pulled out the small tin cup, holding it out to Amos.

The monkey chattered wildly, taking the cup. Lovingly, Amos rubbed his head against the cup, then held it close, like he always did.

"See? It's Amos!" Benny exclaimed.

"I'll tell you what we'll do," Grandfather said to Benny. "We'll come back and bring Edward. He'll be able to claim his monkey."

He faced the clerk. "If I were you, I wouldn't buy that monkey just yet."

"Why are you interfering?" Mac asked nervously, his hands bunching into fists, then opening again. "This is *my* monkey and I intend to sell it!"

The clerk looked from Grandfather to the children and back to Mac Thatcher. "I see no reason not to buy this monkey." He counted out the cash and placed it in Mac's hand.

In horror Violet watched as the clerk took the cage and disappeared into the back room.

"That's all the good it did you to try to stop this sale!" Mac growled, casting a nasty look at Benny and stuffing the money into his back pocket. With a snicker, he stomped out.

The clerk returned, quickly filling Jessie's order.

As they went out, Benny glanced back, whispering, "We'll save you, Amos."

CHAPTER 11

The Guilty One

When Grandfather drove to the zoo, the children piled out, intending to find Edward. Grandfather trailed after them.

"Did Amos come back?" Benny shouted at Edward, who stood before the Monkey House.

Sadly, Edward shook his head. "I'm afraid not. Pat and I have searched the entire grounds, and he's no place to be found."

"*I* know where he is!" Benny said.

Edward gave him a sharp look. "You do? Where is he?"

"Mac Thatcher sold him to the pet shop man," Benny answered, his eyes fastened on Edward.

"Can you believe Mac Thatcher could have stolen Amos?" Henry asked.

"Yes, I can," Edward said in a discouraged tone.

"You don't seem surprised," Violet said.

"I'm not," Edward said dully.

The children and Grandfather waited patiently for Edward's explanation.

"I'll tell you about Mac Thatcher later," Edward said. "First let's go see if the pet shop monkey is mine."

"Yes, yes," Benny said so excited that he ran from Edward to Grandfather. "Amos was stuffed in a real little cage and we've got to get him out!"

"And we will," Edward said grimly.

Pat, who came out of the Bird House, joined them, and Edward quickly told her about Mac Thatcher and the monkey.

"Oh, no," she groaned. "I thought we'd seen the last of him."

Edward started walking toward the exit.

"I'm going to Bridgeport. Hopefully Amos is still at the pet shop."

Jessie handed Pat the box of vitamins and special food. "Here's what you asked for."

"Thanks, Jessie," Pat said, rewarding her with a warm smile. "I'll see to it that the black panther gets his vitamins."

"And you know which other animals need their food," Edward called over his shoulder.

"Yes," Pat answered, a worried frown crossing her forehead. "You run along." She gave Benny a quick pat on the back. "I'm sure Amos will be there."

"I know it!" Benny responded promptly, hurrying to catch up with Edward.

So back to Bridgeport they drove, this time with Edward in the front seat.

Once inside the pet shop, the clerk took one look at the children and hurried to the rear to get the monkey.

Returning, he set the cage on the counter where Edward could examine the monkey.

In a few minutes Edward announced, in a triumphant burst, "It's Amos!"

"I knew it!" Benny said gleefully.

"I paid five hundred dollars for that monkey," the clerk sniffed, "and I don't intend to give him up."

"Well, I'm buying him back at the same price," Edward said sternly. "This monkey was kidnapped from my zoo. I recognize him from that brown marking on his head."

"Oh, my," the clerk said. "If you'll pay me the money, I'll be grateful. I don't want any trouble by dealing with a stolen monkey!"

Edward wrote out the check, mumbling, "I'll take this out of Mac Thatcher's hide!"

Benny talked to Amos, and the bright-eyed monkey responded by chattering and sticking out a paw.

Violet leaned down to the cage and said softly, "You're going home now, Amos."

"Not quite to the zoo yet," Edward said grimly. He turned to the white-faced clerk. "May I use your telephone?"

"Help yourself."

Dialing the Rosedale police, he told them a few things that had happened at the zoo and asked them to meet him at Mac Thatcher's house, giving them the address.

Henry wondered how he knew Mac's address.

"Let's go to Mac Thatcher's, James," Edward said, his face a thundercloud. "Now Mac will pay for what he's done."

The children scrambled into the station wagon. Benny sat in the very back with Amos. Jessie tried to piece together what had happened, but decided she'd better be patient and ask Edward later.

Grandfather, not losing a minute, drove out of the parking space and headed back to Rosedale. If he'd had a siren, it would have been going full blast.

"How do you know where Mac Thatcher lives?" Jessie ventured to ask.

"Oh, I know a lot about Mac," Edward said. "You see, he used to work for me. He was a lazy worker, often forgetting to feed the animals. Or he'd be late for work, neglecting his tasks."

Henry nodded. "That sounds like Mac. We were in his bookstore, and he hadn't fed Scamper, either."

"Scamper?" Edward questioned.

"Scamper's a cute little dog," Benny explained. "If we didn't have Watch, I'd like to take him home."

"He is a sweet dog," Jessie added. "You could tell by the way Mac treated him that he didn't get any attention or love."

Edward continued, "I just couldn't have an employee who was irresponsible with my animals." His eyes flashed, remembering. "He didn't even like animals. A zoo is no place for a person who dislikes animals."

"That's terrible!" Violet whispered, her face stricken.

Entering Rosedale, Edward directed, "Turn left at the light, James. Anyway, I fired Mac," he continued, "and hired Pat."

"I can see why," Henry said.

"You can't have someone unreliable working with animals," Edward said. "He not only forgot to feed some of them, but he didn't clean out their homes, either." He shook his head. "If you work with animals, you must be very responsible."

"I wonder if Mac emptied the seals' pool

and changed temperatures, and did all those other mean things?" Violet asked.

"Well, he was angry with me for firing him, but we have no proof that he did those other things," Edward replied. "One thing for sure, though, is that he's going to answer for stealing Amos! He took him because he just wanted to get back at me any way he could." He pointed. "Third house on the left, James."

Suddenly, Mac dashed out carrying a suitcase. He opened the trunk of his car.

Turning, he saw the Aldens and Edward. He pressed his lips together and waited for them to get out of the car.

"What do you want now?" he sneered, folding his arms across his chest. "You follow me to the pet shop and now you follow me to my house!"

"I think you know why we're here," Edward said calmly, his eyes never leaving Mac's frowning face.

"You stole Amos and sold him to the pet shop!" Benny said in an accusing tone. "We saw you!"

"No, I didn't," Mac retorted, an edge to his voice. "That monkey was nothing but trouble. Why would I want to steal him?"

"For the money," Edward said shortly. "We went to the pet shop and rescued Amos. The monkey is in the station wagon. I've positively identified him! And," he added, "the clerk can positively identify *you*!"

Mac glanced at the car and saw Amos in the cage. "Okay, so I tried to sell your monkey," he admitted. "I didn't get much money for him." He shot Edward a hateful look. "After all, I lost my job and my salary!"

Edward calmly replied, "You deserved to be let go, Mac Thatcher, and I think you know it. I wouldn't put it past you to have drained the seals' pool, changed the temperatures, and stolen my files!"

Mac gritted his teeth in annoyance. "Well, I didn't do it! All I did was take a measly monkey."

Doubtfully, Jessie stared at Mac. She didn't like his mean little eyes and narrow dark face. But she realized that didn't make him guilty.

"Did you change all the names of the animals?" Benny asked.

Mac looked surprised. "What do you mean?"

"The giraffes' sign was put in front of the bears, and the monkeys' sign was in front of the elephants," Violet explained.

Mac snorted. "I never heard of such a thing!" Abruptly, he yanked the keys out of the trunk, and they dropped in the street.

"Wait a minute!" Edward shouted, scooping up the keys, and dangling them before Mac's eyes. "Why do you have my zoo office key and the key to the gates?"

"I forgot to turn in the fool things," Mac said stiffly, but he bit his lip in confusion.

"I don't think so," Edward said icily. "You *did* turn in your keys, but first you had a second set made. This explains how you got into the zoo. You knew all about the zoo's wires, how to change the temperature, and where the files were kept, didn't you?"

Sullen, Mac stared at the ground.

"We saw you several times at the zoo, too," Henry said. "Now we know why."

"Yes," Benny said, nodding his head vigorously, "and you asked us a lot of questions about the zoo!" He stuck out his chin, daring Mac to contradict him.

Mac's eyes shifted from one to the other, then back to the telltale keys.

"All right!" Mac growled. "I guess you've got me. Sure I did all the things you mentioned! Why shouldn't I?" Mac paused, his eyes narrowing. "You had it coming! No one fires Mac Thatcher and gets away with it. I'd be happy if your zoo closed."

"You hurt the animals!" Benny said, his disbelieving eyes opening wide.

"If it hadn't been for you kids and that mangy monkey, you'd never be the wiser." He snatched the keys from Edward's hands. "But try and stop me! I'm leaving Rosedale forever!"

Suddenly, a police car pulled up and two policemen jumped out.

Quickly, Edward told the police lieutenant the story of his animals and what had been done to them. "I'm sure the files will be in the house."

The first policeman arrested Mac and ordered him into the back of the squad car. The lieutenant entered the house with Edward and the Aldens. Sure enough, the files were stacked in a corner.

Henry and Jessie picked up the important papers and carried them out to the car.

Scamper dashed outside with them, then stood on his hind legs.

"Who will take care of Scamper?" Benny wailed. "If Mac goes to jail, there won't be anyone to feed him."

Edward reached down and scratched the dog under its chin. Scamper eagerly licked his fingers. "Well, Scamper, it looks like you'll be coming home with me. I'd like a little fellow like you around the house."

"Oh, good," Violet said, petting Scamper.

The dog looked at them with his big dark eyes. He obviously wanted someone to love and to be loved himself.

Edward found a leash and fastened it to Scamper's collar and led him outdoors. "By the way, officer, Mac Thatcher owes me five hundred dollars. That's the money he made when he stole my monkey from the zoo and sold him."

"Come down to the station in a few hours and swear out a complaint," the officer said, "and we'll see that you get your money."

"Thanks, officer," Edward said, with a wave. After the police car left, he breathed a sigh of relief. He turned to the Aldens and the old twinkle crept back into his eyes. "To the zoo, James!"

Arriving at the gates, Edward immediately let Scamper out, holding onto the leash, and with his other hand took the cage to the Monkey House and opened it. At first the monkey stood quite still, then suddenly he erupted into a ball of energy. He leapt up, grabbed the trapeze and swung wildly back and forth. Then he grasped a tree branch and climbed to the top.

As they watched the monkey, a high-pitched voice interrupted them. "Yoo-hoo, Edward Marlow."

In dismay the children turned and saw Helen Brooks bearing down on them, her high heels clicking determinedly.

Not Helen Brooks, Violet thought, her heart skipping a beat. In the joy of finding Amos and uncovering Mac Thatcher, she'd almost forgotten the woman who wanted to close the zoo. But now here was Helen Brooks to ruin the day.

CHAPTER 12

A Change of Heart

Helen Brooks faced Edward Marlow.

"Hello, Helen," Edward greeted her coolly.

"I hear your zoo has been having lots of problems," Helen said. "You can't keep the animals quiet if something is bothering them!"

"Yes," Edward admitted. "But we've found the one responsible for the zoo's troubles."

"I knew something was going on," she said

smugly. "What I want to know is are these troubles really over?" She shook a red fingernail under Edward's nose.

"The troubles are over," Edward said calmly. Then he glared at her. "Except for *you*, Helen."

Helen drew herself up and straightened her purple hat. "You don't need to worry about me any longer."

"What do you mean?" Henry asked. "Aren't you trying to close Edward's zoo?"

"Not anymore," Helen said, lifting her chin and pressing her lips into a thin line.

Edward's eyes opened wide. "You mean you're not bringing this before the town council?"

"Actually, no," Helen said, gazing down at her oversized purse. "You see, I had a talk with my fellow council members, and they informed me that they'd *never* vote to close the zoo. They said it gave too much pleasure to the people of Rosedale." She met Edward's eyes. "I know when I'm defeated."

Edward grabbed Helen's hand and shook it up and down. "Thank you! Thank you!"

"And you know I've often sat in my car in front of the zoo to see if I could find something wrong." Helen managed a smile. "The only thing I saw were a lot of happy faces."

"That's great news, Miss Brooks," Violet said shyly. "The zoo is really a wonderful place."

Helen glanced at Violet. "Yes, it is, dear," she murmured.

"I'm glad you don't want to close the zoo," Benny said, grinning at her.

"You know something," Helen said. "I'm glad, too."

They told Helen good-bye, and Grandfather said, "We've got to say good-bye, too."

"Yes, Watch and Mrs. McGregor will wonder what happened to us," Jessie said.

"I'm so glad you don't have to worry about the zoo being closed," Violet said, a smile lighting her pretty face.

"So am I!" Edward said emphatically.

"Surely you'll be able to stay one more day," Edward said.

"Yes, there are a few odds and ends I need to clean up in the yard," Grandfather said.

"Besides, I know my grandchildren would enjoy one more day at the zoo — a day without problems."

"Yes, oh, yes," Jessie said, bending down to scratch Scamper behind the ears.

"You bet we would," Henry echoed.

Their last morning, over a breakfast of pancakes and sausages, Jessie asked Edward, "Do you think we could have a party tonight and invite Pat and David?"

"We want to make dinner for you one last time," Violet said, smiling.

"That's a splendid idea!" Edward said. "I'll ask Pat and David today."

"Should we ask anyone else?" Henry asked.

"Who would it be?" Benny wanted to know.

"Are you thinking of Helen Brooks?" Jessie said, her eyes twinkling.

Edward thought about it, then said, "Why not? Yesterday she made me very happy. And even though she doesn't know it, she made the animals happy, also!" He rose. "I'll see you children at the zoo." And he went out the door.

The Aldens bought groceries and cooked all morning.

In the afternoon the children walked to the zoo for the last time. They visited each of the animals. Benny spent the longest time at the Monkey House. He laughed at Amos's funny tricks, but when it was time to go, his smile vanished. Waving at Amos, he stepped away. "I'll be back," he promised.

That night, when everyone plus Pat, Helen Brooks, and David were seated at the candlelit table, the children served dinner.

David's eyes grew big when he saw the dishes of delicious roast turkey, dressing, mashed potatoes and gravy, cranberry sauce, and buttered peas set on a white tablecloth. Later, apple pie and ice cream was served for dessert.

Cleaning his plate, Edward leaned back with a contented look on his face. When Helen Brooks smiled, Benny thought she looked almost pretty. "You should smile more often," he blurted out.

Helen's mouth opened in astonishment, then she winked. "I know I should. When you were kind enough to invite me to dinner, I promised myself I'd be more pleasant." Her blue dress brought out the blue of her eyes, and, as she carefully folded her napkin, she murmured, "I'm ashamed of the way I acted." She glanced around the table. "I'm surprised you're speaking to me."

Everyone was pleased that the evening was such a happy occasion, and after the guests had left, the children, Edward, and Grandfather went into the living room. Edward settled into his easy chair next to his bookcase and cabinet. The children were proud of the cozy corner they had made for him.

Henry poured Grandfather and Edward another cup of coffee, then sat on the floor next to Jessie and Violet. Benny perched on the arm of Grandfather's chair. They discussed the zoo and all the things that had happened to the animals. They talked about Mac Thatcher and poor kidnapped Amos, and Helen Brooks, and the fun they'd had.

Jessie, sitting cross-legged, glanced up at

Edward. "We had a wonderful time!"

"So did I," Edward said, reaching down and stroking Scamper, who lay at his feet. "I'll miss you when you leave, but I hope you'll come back."

"Oh, we will." Grandfather laughed. "I need to check on the roses and new shrubs."

Benny yawned. "I'm sleepy," he admitted.

"Yes, it's time to go to bed," Violet said, standing and stretching.

Grandfather said, "We're leaving early, children, so get a good night's sleep."

It had been a wonderful vacation, full of fun and mystery, but now it was over and time to go home. They could hardly wait to tell Mrs. McGregor all about it.

GERTRUDE CHANDLER WARNER discovered when she was teaching that many readers who like an exciting story could find no books that were both easy and fun to read. She decided to try to meet this need, and her first book, *The Boxcar Children*, quickly proved she had succeeded.

Miss Warner drew on her own experiences to write each mystery. As a child she spent hours watching trains go by on the tracks opposite her family home. She often dreamed about what it would be like to set up housekeeping in a caboose or freight car — the situation the Alden children find themselves in.

When Miss Warner received requests for more adventures involving Henry, Jessie, Violet, and Benny Alden, she began additional stories. In each, she chose a special setting and introduced unusual or eccentric characters who like the unpredictable.

While the mystery element is central to each of Miss Warner's books, she never thought of them as strictly juvenile mysteries. She liked to stress the Aldens' independence and resourcefulness and their solid New England devotion to using up and making do. The Aldens go about most of their adventures with as little adult supervision as possible — something else that delights young readers.

Miss Warner lived in Putnam, Connecticut, until her death in 1979. During her lifetime, she received hundreds of letters from girls and boys telling her how much they liked her books.